FOR THE LOVE OF SPORTS

VOLLEYBALL

Natasha Evdokimoff

AV² provides enriched content that supplements and complements this book. Weigl's AV² books strive to create inspired learning and engage young minds in a total learning experience.

Your AV² Media Enhanced books come alive with...

Audio
Listen to sections of the book read aloud.

Key Words
Study vocabulary, and complete a matching word activity.

Go to www.av2books.com, and enter this book's unique code.

Video
Watch informative video clips.

Quizzes
Test your knowledge.

BOOK CODE

AVD27795

Embedded Weblinks
Gain additional information for research.

Slide Show
View images and captions, and prepare a presentation.

AV² by Weigl brings you media enhanced books that support active learning.

Try This!
Complete activities and hands-on experiments.

... and much, much more!

Published by AV² by Weigl
350 5th Avenue, 59th Floor
New York, NY 10118
Website: www.av2books.com

Library of Congress Control Number: 2018965252

ISBN   978-1-7911-0029-2 (hardcover)
ISBN   978-1-7911-0569-3 (softcover)
ISBN   978-1-7911-0030-8 (multi-user eBook)
ISBN   978-1-7911-0031-5 (single-user eBook)

Printed in the United States of America in Brainerd, Minnesota
1 2 3 4 5 6 7 8 9 0   22 21 20 19 18

122018
103118

Project Coordinator: John Willis
Art Director: Terry Paulhus

Photo Credits
Every reasonable effort has been made to trace ownership and to obtain permission to reprint copyright material. The publishers would be pleased to have any errors or omissions brought to their attention so that they may be corrected in subsequent printings.

Weigl acknowledges Alamy, Getty Images, and Wikimedia as its primary image suppliers for this title.

FOR THE LOVE OF SPORTS

VOLLEYBALL

CONTENTS

What Is Volleyball?

Volleyball was invented by William Morgan in 1895. During a trial game, someone said that the ball was "volleyed" over the net. The game then became known as volleyball. The first game was played at Massachusetts College in 1896. For the first few years, players used a basketball. By 1900, a special ball was designed just for volleyball.

In 1930, the first official outdoor game was played. Outdoor volleyball can be played on grass, but it is most often played on sand. Beach volleyball has developed its own rules and leagues.

By 1900, volleyball was a popular sport for both men and women.

In volleyball, two teams of six stand on opposite sides of a raised net. Players keep a ball in the air by hitting or passing it. Most often the ball is hit with hands, wrists, or arms. To score, a team must get the ball to touch the ground on the other side of the net within the boundary lines. Volleyball has leagues for men and women at all levels. Different rules sometimes apply to different leagues. More than 800 million people play this sport around the world every week.

Today, more than 46 million people play volleyball in the United States.

Volleyball has been part of the **Summer Olympics** since 1964.

The average male volleyball player is between **6 feet 1 inch** (1.85 meters) and **6 feet 11 inches** (2.1 m) tall.

Division I schools offer **330** women's volleyball **scholarships** each year.

Getting Ready to Play

A volleyball weighs between 9 and 10 ounces (255 and 283 grams).

A volleyball player's uniform must be light so the player can jump and move fast. It does not take much equipment to play volleyball.

A volleyball is made of soft, padded leather. The leather is stitched over rubber, and the ball is filled with air. The ball is very light, so hitting it with arms and wrists does not hurt. Volleyballs are usually white, but can be brightly colored for beach games.

In volleyball, players sometimes tip the ball over the net. This tricky move can often score points.

A net separates the two teams. A volleyball net is made of **mesh**. The corners are tied to poles to pull the net tight. For adult players, the net is more than 7 feet (2.1 m) high. For junior players, it stands just below 7 feet (2.1 m). Two flexible rods called **antennas** stick up at both ends of the net. These rods help show if the ball goes out of bounds while going over the net.

Beach volleyball players do not wear shoes or knee pads. The sand provides a soft surface to land on.

Players usually wear T-shirts. Some players like to wear long sleeves to cushion their arms. Team members all wear the same color. Every player wears a number so the officials can make calls easily.

Players often wear a pair of gym shorts to play. They are comfortable so players can move quickly and easily.

Players wear pads on their knees and sometimes on their elbows. Pads help to prevent injuries when players dive on the floor for the ball.

A pair of good sneakers is important for this game. Sneakers have rubber soles to help prevent slipping when players jump and move for the ball.

The Court

Volleyball is played on a rectangular court. Boundary lines around the court show its area. The boundary lines are called sidelines and end lines. To score a point, the ball must land inside the boundary. The area outside the boundary is called the **free zone**. If the ball lands in the free zone, it is out of play. Only the **serving** team can score points.

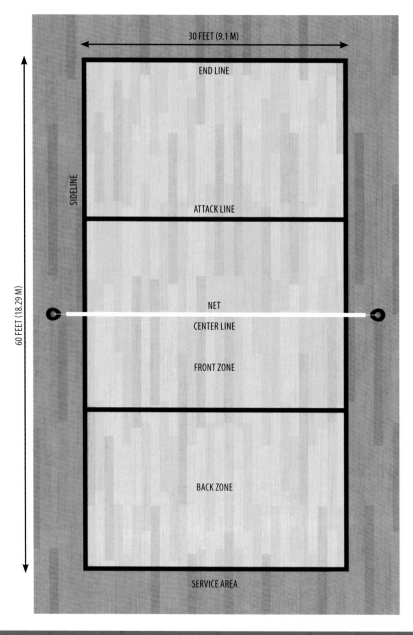

Volleyball Tournaments

USA Volleyball hosts tournaments at the highest level for both indoor and outdoor volleyball. Many beaches all over the United States host tournaments each spring and summer. For indoor volleyball, fans can watch **matches** between the 40 U.S. regional teams.

Members of the Association of Volleyball Professionals (AVP) compete each year during the King of the Court Crown Series. Top players can make between $7,500 and $15,000. In 2018, the tournament took place on Huntington Beach, California.

Order on the Court

The court is divided into two equal sides by the center line. The net hangs directly above the center line. Teams switch sides of the playing court after every game. Each side of the court has two zones. One is the **front zone** and the other is the **back zone**. The **attack line** separates these zones and shows where players should stand. Players do different jobs depending on which zone they stand in.

A volleyball event is called a match. There are often three or five games in a match. The team that wins the most games in the match wins. In most games, the first team to score 15 points wins. A team must win by two points in regular games. To score points, the server hits the ball over the net. If it touches the ground on the other side within the boundary, the serving team scores one point.

Volleyball players make signals behind their backs to tell their teammates which moves to make on the court.

If the serve goes out of bounds or does not make it over the net, the team loses possession. If the ball touches the ground on the serving team's side in a **rally**, the team loses the serve. No points are scored when this happens. Instead, a **side out** is called, and the other team takes a turn at serving.

Teams can hit the ball only three times when it is on their side. Players must send the ball back over the net by the third hit. A player cannot hit the ball twice in a row. Players could originally hit the ball only with their upper bodies. A 1996 rule change made it legal to play the ball off the players' lower bodies.

Not all leagues follow this ruling. If a player briefly catches or **carries** the ball, it is called a **fault**. Some other faults are crossing the center line and touching the net. If the serving team faults, it loses the serve. If the receiving team faults, the serving team scores a point.

Every match has two referees and two line judges. The first referee sits on a raised platform at one end of the net. This gives him or her a clear view of the entire court. The second referee stands on the floor at the other end of the net to watch for low violations.

Referees make sure the game's rules are followed. The line judges stand in the free zone on opposite ends and sides of the court. Their job is to decide if the ball lands in or out of bounds. Line judges use flags to show their calls.

Teammates must position the ball for each other to get it over the net because the same player cannot touch the ball twice in a row. This requires a great deal of teamwork.

Positions

Teams are made up of six players who stand in two rows. Three stand in the front zone, and three stand in the back zone.

Players in the front zone jump at the net to **block** hard hits. They also **spike** the ball onto the other team's side. Back-zone players receive serves from the other team. They also **bump** the ball to front-zone players, who then try to score.

The server stands at the back of the court, usually to the right. The server steps behind the end line with the ball. He or she then hits the ball overhand or underhand over the net. This means using the hand to hit the top or bottom of the ball. If the server steps over the line, the referee calls a foot foul, and the team loses its serve. Once the ball is served, the player can step back in bounds.

SERVER

Players serve by tossing the ball in the air with one hand and hitting it with the other hand.

Team members pass the ball between each other as they like, up to three times. A **set** is when a player passes the ball lightly off his or her fingertips to another team member. With this move, the ball can be pushed high in the air. A set is also called a volley. A bump is bounced off a player's extended forearms. Bumps are best to pass low balls or return hard serves or spikes.

Liberos are substitute players. They can pass and dig up hits, but they cannot jump at the net. They are strictly defensive players.

Unlike other athletes, most volleyball players play every position. Teams **rotate** positions in a clockwise direction on the court. They rotate whenever the team gets a new turn to serve.

OUTSIDE HITTER

The outside hitter stands on either the right or the left side of the court. The setter sets up the outside hitter. A good set allows the outside hitter to spike fast and well.

The two front-zone players try to block spiked balls from crossing the net. Some blockers reach well over the net and into the opponent's court.

BLOCKER

Making It Big

Volleyball teams start at the junior high or high school level. There are girls' and boys' teams in grades 7 through 12. Schools play against each other through the season, competing for the city title.

There are many regional volleyball clubs for young players. Club leagues have teams for girls and boys between 7 and 18 years old.

There, players learn the skills they will need for highly competitive play. After high school, many players choose to play on college or university teams. These games are fast paced and fun to watch. Colleges and universities from across the country compete for the national college title.

Playing volleyball outside has been popular for many years. Outdoor games got started in California and were often played on the beach. Groups of people would make teams and enjoy the game as part of a fun day outside. Soon, beach games became competitive.

Many high school volleyball players in the United States start out playing on a junior varsity team, and advance to varsity as they improve.

Volleyball players spend many hours practicing to become good at the sport.

At first, the same rules were used for both indoor and outdoor games. Before long, beach volleyball started a separate league with its own rules. In most beach games, there are only two players per team playing on a sand court. Two-person teams guarantee the action will be fast and exciting.

All serious players would love to represent their country on an Olympic volleyball team. Both indoor and beach volleyball are played at the Summer Olympic Games. Teams from around the world play intense matches in competition for the gold medal.

Professional teams get paid to play volleyball. Beach volleyball has professional men's and women's teams. The United States has a professional indoor volleyball league as well.

Beach volleyball players wear bathing suits and other stretchy clothes to help keep sand off. Because they are in the sun, players often wear sunglasses or visors. Courts are made with soft sand, so no shoes or pads are needed. Today, there are professional beach volleyball leagues all over the world. Players earn prize money for winning games.

One of the oldest and most important Fédération Internationale de Volleyball (FIVB) events is the Volleyball World Championship.

Success in international competitions, such as the Olympics, is a major accomplishment. Jen Kessy won a silver medal at the 2012 London Olympics.

History of Volleyball

Volleyball has transformed from a beloved backyard game to a sport world-renowned athletes compete in. Beach volleyball has become very popular during the Summer Olympics. Indoor volleyball is played at the highest level in 330 universities in the United States.

During the 2016 Summer Olympics, the U.S. men's volleyball team came in third and earned a bronze medal.

1895  Volleyball is invented by William G. Morgan. It is designed to combine basketball, baseball, tennis, and handball.

1928 The United States Volleyball Association, which later became USA Volleyball, is formed. This organization regulates volleyball rules and plans official tournaments.

1964 During the Tokyo Olympics, men's and women's teams can medal in volleyball for the first time.

1996 Beach volleyball becomes an Olympic sport during the Summer Olympics in Atlanta, Georgia.

2016 Kerri Walsh Jennings becomes the first U.S. player to compete in four Olympic beach volleyball tournaments. She wins a bronze medal along with her teammate, April Ross.

2018 Poland defeats Brazil to win the 2018 FIVB Volleyball Men's World Championship for the second time in a row.

The **first** name for volleyball was **mintonette**, which is French for "volleyball."

The first volleyball net was only **6 feet 6 inches** (2 m) high.

The first documented use of **setting** a ball and then spiking it happened in the Philippines in **1916**.

Superstars of Volleyball

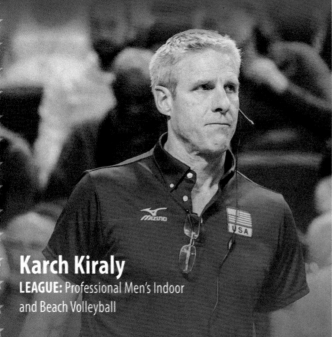

These are some of the well-known players of this exciting sport's history.

Karch Kiraly

LEAGUE: Professional Men's Indoor and Beach Volleyball

CAREER FACTS:
- In 1984, Kiraly was the youngest member of the men's Olympic indoor volleyball team.
- Kiraly was the Olympic indoor team captain in 1988. The team won the gold medal. With Kiraly's help, the indoor team won two more gold medals, making Kiraly the only player in Olympic volleyball history to win three gold medals.
- In 1996, Kiraly won Olympic gold in the beach volleyball competition.
- Kiraly won more tournaments and money than any other player on the AVP Pro Beach Volleyball Tour in his 27 seasons. He won more than $3.1 million playing beach volleyball.
- Kiraly was inducted into the Volleyball Hall of Fame in 2001.

Kerri Walsh Jennings

LEAGUE: Professional Women's Beach Volleyball

CAREER FACTS:
- Walsh was considered to be one of the top all-around players in college volleyball. She had 1,553 **kills**, 1,285 digs, and 502 blocks during her time at Stanford.
- At the 2004 Olympics in Athens, Walsh and Misty May-Treanor won gold in women's beach volleyball. They won every game at the Olympics.
- Walsh enjoyed a winning streak of 89 matches from 2003 to 2004.
- At both the 2008 and 2012 Olympics, Walsh Jennings and May-Treanor won gold medals in women's beach volleyball.
- Walsh is married to Casey Jennings. Casey is one of the best men's volleyball players in the world.

Flora Jean "Flo" Hyman

LEAGUE: Professional Women's Indoor Volleyball

CAREER FACTS:
- Hyman was a three-time All-American at the University of Houston from 1974 to 1976.
- She was chosen to be on many all-star teams.
- Hyman was named the Best Attacker at the Pan-Am Games in 1975, 1979, and 1983.
- Hyman was also named as the Best Attacker at the World University Games in 1973 and 1977.
- Hyman helped lead the U.S. national women's indoor volleyball team to win a silver medal at the 1984 Olympic Games in Los Angeles.
- Hyman has been awarded many honors since her death in 1986, including being inducted to the Volleyball Hall of Fame in 1988.

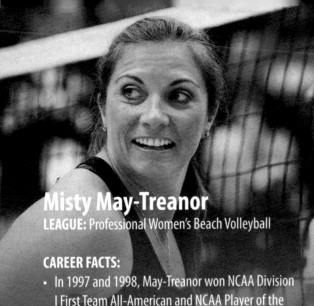

Misty May-Treanor

LEAGUE: Professional Women's Beach Volleyball

CAREER FACTS:
- In 1997 and 1998, May-Treanor won NCAA Division I First Team All-American and NCAA Player of the Year. She was inducted into the Long Beach State Athletics Hall of Fame in 2004.
- In 2000, May-Treanor was voted as one of the top six volleyball players in NCAA history.
- In 2003, May-Treanor began playing with Walsh Jennings in the AVP Pro Beach Volleyball Tour. They were voted "Best Team" in 2003, after a 9–0 season. They received the same honor for the next three years.
- At the 2004, 2008, and 2012 Olympics, May-Treanor and Walsh Jennings won gold medals in beach volleyball.

Gabrielle Reece

LEAGUE: Professional Women's Beach Volleyball

CAREER FACTS:
- Reece attended Florida State University, where she set the university record for most blocks, with 747.
- In 1994 and 1995, Reece was the Offensive Player of the Year.
- Reece was captain of her team for five seasons.
- Reece was the leader in game kills from 1994 to 1996.

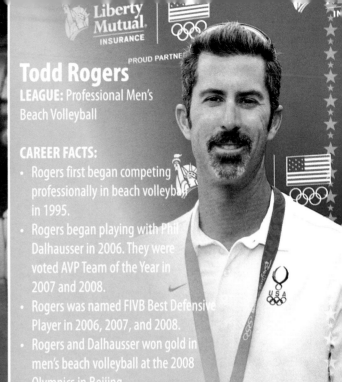

Todd Rogers

LEAGUE: Professional Men's Beach Volleyball

CAREER FACTS:
- Rogers first began competing professionally in beach volleyball in 1995.
- Rogers began playing with Phil Dalhausser in 2006. They were voted AVP Team of the Year in 2007 and 2008.
- Rogers was named FIVB Best Defensive Player in 2006, 2007, and 2008.
- Rogers and Dalhausser won gold in men's beach volleyball at the 2008 Olympics in Beijing.

Sinjin Smith

LEAGUE: Professional Men's Beach Volleyball

CAREER FACTS:
- Smith played beach volleyball at UCLA. With Smith's help, UCLA won two national championships in 1976 and 1979.
- Smith was on the U.S. national team from 1979 to 1982.
- Smith was named the AVP Best Defensive Player in 1990, 1991, and 1992.
- Smith and partner Randy Stoklos were FIVB tour champions in 1989, 1990, 1991, and 1992.
- Smith was inducted into the Volleyball Hall of Fame in 2003.

Staying Healthy

A healthy diet helps people be strong athletes. Fruits and vegetables provide many of the vitamins people need. Breads, pasta, and rice are sources of food energy. Meats have protein for building muscles. Dairy products have calcium, which keeps bones strong. Eating foods from all the food groups every day will keep a player's body in top condition.

Drinking plenty of water before, during, and after playing sports is important. Water keeps people's bodies cool and running well. When athletes sweat, they lose water. Water replaces what is lost through sweat during a game.

Drinking plenty of water before, during, and after playing sports is important.

Pasta is a good source of carbohydrates. Carbohydrates provide the body much of the energy it needs to keep active and healthy.

Strong and flexible muscles are important for playing well. Training the right muscles a few times every week makes playing more fun and helps prevent injuries. Stretching keeps muscles flexible. It is best to stretch after a **warm-up**. Running in place for a few minutes or doing some laps gets muscles warm.

Strong legs are needed for quick movements. For strong legs, players practice jumping in place. They pull their knees up as high as they can on each jump. Lunges are other great exercises for stretching leg muscles. Standing with their feet slightly apart, players shift their weight to one side and bend their knee. The other leg stays straight and stretches out.

Players need strong hands and fingers, too. To work these muscles, they squeeze a tennis ball in each hand several times. Players also stretch their shoulder muscles to prepare for hitting and passing the ball.

It is important to always be careful when stretching to avoid pulling muscles.

- 1 -
Who **invented** volleyball?

- 2 -
When was volleyball invented?

- 3 -
In indoor volleyball, **how many players** from each team stand on opposite sides of the net?

- 4 -
How many people play volleyball in the **United States**?

THE VOLLEYBALL QUIZ

- 5 -
What does the **net** hang directly above?

- 6 -
What is a **volleyball event** called?

- 7 -
In indoor games, how many players from one team stand in the **back zone**?

- 8 -
Where did the first **two-man** beach volleyball tournament take place?

- 9 -
When did beach volleyball first become an **Olympic sport**?

- 10 -
During the **2016 Summer Olympics**, which medal did the U.S. Men's Volleyball team earn?

ANSWERS: **1** William Morgan **2** 1895 **3** Six **4** 46 million **5** The center line **6** A match **7** Three **8** Los Angeles **9** 1996 **10** Bronze

Key Words

antennas: flexible rods on the net that help show when the ball goes out of bounds

attack line: the line that divides the front and back zones

back zone: the area between the attack and end line

block: when players jump up at the net to stop a hard spike from the other team

bump: a pass where the ball contacts the forearms; arms are straight and hands are joined

carries: holds the ball instead of letting it bounce quickly off the fingertips

fault: an illegal move or play called by an official

free zone: the area outside the end lines and sidelines

front zone: the court area between the attack line and center line

kills: strong hits that result in points; usually done by spiking the ball

matches: series of three or five games

mesh: fine rope linked together forming a loose kind of screen

rally: a series of hits over the net between teams

rotate: clockwise movement teams make before serving the ball; occurs after a side out is called

serving: hitting the ball overhand or underhand over the net from behind the end line

set: a soft hit with the fingertips that sends the ball high into the air so another player can spike it

side out: the call made when the serving team commits a fault, causing it to lose the right to serve

spike: a hard, downward hit made above the net, aimed at the opponent's side of the court

warm-up: gentle exercise to get the body ready for stretching and game play

Index

Log on to www.av2books.com

AV² by Weigl brings you media enhanced books that support active learning. Go to www.av2books.com, and enter the special code found on page 2 of this book. You will gain access to enriched and enhanced content that supplements and complements this book. Content includes video, audio, weblinks, quizzes, a slide show, and activities.

AV² Online Navigation

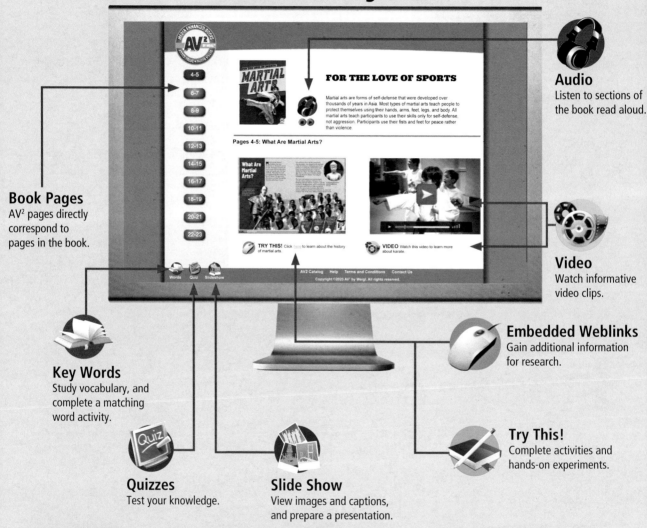

Book Pages
AV² pages directly correspond to pages in the book.

Key Words
Study vocabulary, and complete a matching word activity.

Quizzes
Test your knowledge.

Slide Show
View images and captions, and prepare a presentation.

Audio
Listen to sections of the book read aloud.

Video
Watch informative video clips.

Embedded Weblinks
Gain additional information for research.

Try This!
Complete activities and hands-on experiments.

AV² was built to bridge the gap between print and digital. We encourage you to tell us what you like and what you want to see in the future.

Sign up to be an AV² Ambassador at www.av2books.com/ambassador.

Due to the dynamic nature of the Internet, some of the URLs and activities provided as part of AV² by Weigl may have changed or ceased to exist. AV² by Weigl accepts no responsibility for any such changes. All media enhanced books are regularly monitored to update addresses and sites in a timely manner. Contact AV² by Weigl at 1-866-649-3445 or av2books@weigl.com with any questions, comments, or feedback.